To Zak and Max,
our inspiration x2.

This book was created to help teach children why we wear masks and why it is important that we all make this small effort. Whether we are healthy or weak, young or old, when we wear our mask, we tell everyone we care about them and their loved ones.

About the Author

Lizy Toth believes in dream big, try your hardest, see where it takes you! She happily lives with her husband and her twin boys.

About the Illustrator

Chris Toth is a Creative Director and Illustrator that believes a smile can make all the difference and the phrase "United We Stand" has never been more true than today.

The Love
Behind
The Mask

Written by Lizy Toth
Illustrated by Chris Toth

I am usually a happy kid.
I love to laugh and make silly faces.

But today I was feeling a little sad
or maybe just confused.

When I'm feeling sad my twin brother
always cheers me up. We do everything together.

We were talking about how
much life has changed because
of this crazy virus.

We talk about how much we miss our friends,
how we miss going to school and how we're
missing out on a great soccer season with
our team. We were awesome!

We also talked about how much we miss grandma.

Grandma is the best. She always gives us great big hugs AND she always smells like fresh cookies.

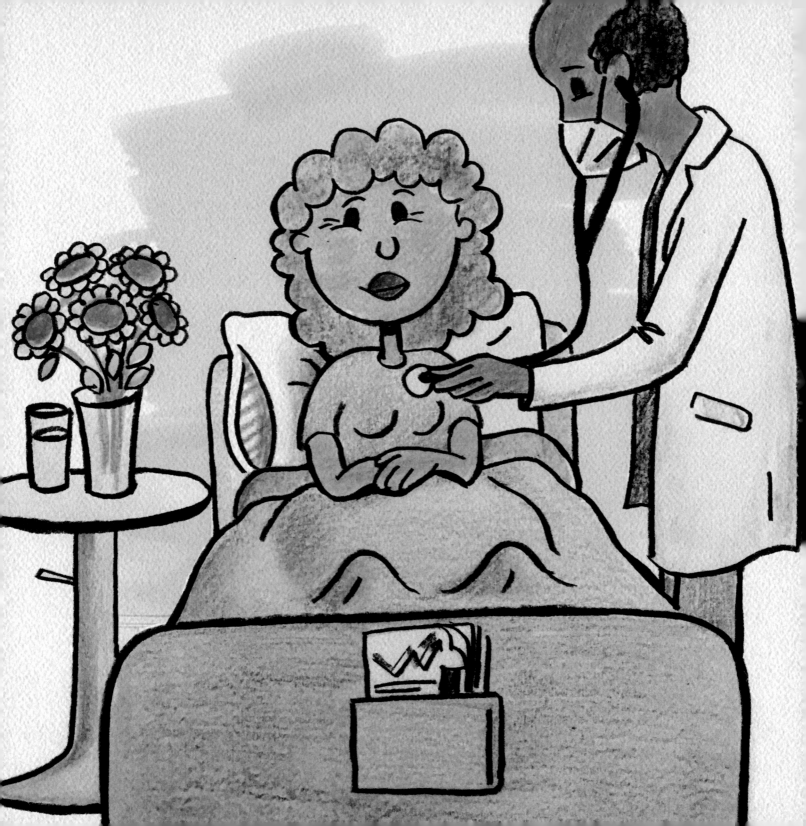

We can't visit her right now because she is sick.

The only people allowed to be with grandma are
the doctors and nurses.

I used to be afraid of doctors and nurses.
Their masks looked scary to me.
But I'm not afraid anymore.

They are working very hard every day to help grandma
get better and the masks protect everyone.

One day we did a video call with grandma. She said it's important for us to help prevent the spread of the virus by:

* Washing our hands with soap and water for at least 2 Happy Birthday songs.

* Keeping our hands out of our mouths, nose and eyes.

* Helping clean things like door knobs, light switches and remote controls.

* Coughing or sneezing into our elbow.

* **And wearing a mask when social distancing is not possible.**

Do you know what **social distancing is?**

It's when you keep at least 6 feet of space between you and people around you outside your home.

My brother and I turned it into a game. It's hilarious.

Today grandma was feeling better and we were allowed to visit her.

We couldn't get close and give her a hug and we had to wear a mask but I know she could feel the love behind the mask.

Grandma was so happy to see us.

So if you see a waiter, teacher or a neighbor wearing a mask, don't be afraid.

It's not scary at all.
They are wearing the mask because they care.
There is love behind the mask.

And if you are asked to wear a mask,
just remember…

You're letting everyone know you care because
there is love behind **your** mask.

I am usually a happy kid.

I love to laugh and make silly faces
and today I am really, really HAPPY.

Grandma finally came home.

The End

Made in the USA
Coppell, TX
19 September 2020